GAMBIT and the
SHADOW KING

adapted by Francine Hughes
based on comic books by Chris Claremont
illustrated by Aristides Ruiz
and Dana and Del Thompson

Random House New York

B ehind the walls of a millionaire's mansion, our drama unfolds. There, the former team leader of the X-Men, Storm, was battling the Shadow King. A sick, evil mutant, the Shadow King could find the worst in a person— the shadow in his or her soul—and twist it into something insidious. Something called…a hound. The Shadow King had set his sights on Storm, and would not rest until he had her in his putrid pack.

No longer a super-strong X-Man, a mutant hero able to command the elements of nature at will, Storm had been trapped in the body of a young girl by the villainous cyborg Nanny. The former X-Man faced the Shadow King and his hounds with the same highly unpredictable powers she had as a child.

Storm summoned all her strength to create a raging blast of wind. It was her only chance.

Outside the mansion, blithely unaware of the chaos inside, a thief was casing the place for a robbery. He was a Cajun, an inhabitant of the Louisiana bayous, called Gambit. He had never

heard of Storm or the X-Men, but he had heard that there was a vault in this mansion filled with valuable stolen paintings.

Gambit found an open window and stepped inside. He stood beside an opulent indoor pool in a room filled with lush green plants.

Sounds of a scuffle and the roar of a vicious wind—*swoosh!*—came from upstairs. A young girl screamed and came crashing over the upstairs railing, plummeting down into the pool. Vile creatures—part human, part beast, and covered with spikes, barked at her from above. *Sacre bleu!* thought Gambit. He didn't know this girl, but clearly she was in trouble. Without hesitating, he pulled her out of the water and dragged her through the house to where he thought the vault would be. Years of thieving made his guess accurate. He picked the lock.

Storm watched silently as Gambit stacked paintings, her thoughts mirroring his. *Who is this person?* Clearly, he was a thief. *Like me,* she thought.

Storm could remember nothing from before

Nanny had turned her into a child. All she knew was how to steal—the way she'd done in her real childhood. It was how she'd been surviving since she'd escaped the evil cyborg's grip, and the reason she'd come to the mansion—to take the priceless paintings. But the paintings had been just bait, used by the Shadow King to lure Storm into his trap. She'd been set up. And for all she knew Gambit was a part of the setup, too. She decided to make a run for it.

Storm was almost to the door—and freedom—when Gambit shouted, "*Attendez, chère!*"

The door burst open. The snarling hounds had tracked her down!

With a magician's sleight-of-hand, Gambit flipped a metal spike out of his sleeve, using his own mutant abilities to charge it with energy. The ordinary piece of metal struck the door with the force of a cannonball.

SKRAMM! The hounds were stunned, and Storm was tossed into Gambit's waiting arms.

"Not your night, eh?" he said. Gambit glanced at the paintings, then back at Storm. "Ah, well,"

he said, carrying Storm out of the vault. "The paintings will keep, *chère.*"

"Stop calling me *chère.* My name is Ororo," she said. "And I don't need your help."

Gambit paid no attention. "I am Gambit," he told her as he moved through the mansion. "And we thieves have to stick together."

They didn't get far. More hounds approached. Gambit set Storm down.

"I can see I'm out of my league," the Cajun said to the hounds in a soft, soothing voice. "A practical man knows his limitations."

The hounds sat quietly on their haunches, drawn into Gambit's web of words. He was charming them into submission.

"Very snappy patter, my friend," a voice boomed down from above, breaking Gambit's spell. It was the Shadow King, on an upstairs landing. "I might put that to use after you've gone through…my reorientation."

Suddenly a searing pain—a mind blast—shot through Gambit's head. The Shadow King grinned. He was about to shoot another blast

when Storm shouted, "Leave him alone!"

"A brave, but foolish, plea," laughed the Shadow King, shifting his attention for a moment to the young girl.

Gambit saw his chance. He grabbed a plate from a nearby table. It sparkled at his touch. The plate was energized. Lethal.

With one swift motion, Gambit flung the plate at the Shadow King like a Frisbee. Contact. *Kaboom!* "After them, hounds!" yelled the Shadow King from amid the rubble.

Storm knew the next move was hers. She sent a gust of wind down the chimney and out the fireplace, sending a cloud of ashes over the room. She grabbed Gambit's hand and led him through the haze.

A minute later, the two were on the roof. "So where do we go from here?" he asked, looking for a way down.

"You hold on to me for dear life," Storm answered, strapping herself into a parachute.

Suddenly a soft breeze was lifting them up, carrying them away. When they reached a

deserted junkyard, Storm gently landed amid piles of scrap metal.

"So this is where you got that parachute," Gambit said, eyeing an abandoned airplane. "Strange place you call home, *chère.*"

"Don't call me that!" Storm said as she led the Cajun inside the plane. "The hounds have tasted my blood, and the Shadow King my thoughts. He will track us down if we don't keep moving."

"I know you can fly on those winds you command," said Gambit. "But lifting a whole airplane may be pushing things."

Storm sat behind the controls, and the plane began to rise on a gust of wind.

"What do you know?" said Gambit, with a smile. He pointed to the river below. "Follow the Big Muddy. *Maman* Mississippi will take us home, *chère.*"

"I *told* you not to…" Storm stopped, speech-less. There was a spaceship hovering in the sky! "I know that ship," she cried. "It's Nanny!"

Just then a hologram of Nanny appeared in the plane, while Nanny's assistant, the Orphan

Maker, snuck on board in person.

"There you are, you naughty girl," the hologram scolded. "Now, you come back to my ship with the Orphan Maker. It's for your own good."

Storm sat transfixed by Nanny as the Orphan Maker advanced.

"Say *bon nuit*, Orphan Maker," Gambit said, tossing an energized metal spike at the assistant and blowing him out the cabin door. The Nanny hologram disappeared.

Storm turned to her new friend with tears in her eyes. "Everyone is after me, Gambit. Why?"

"Because of who you are and what you can do," he told her. "But we are almost home, *chère*. We are almost in New Orleans."

New Orleans! Storm loved the sights and sounds and smells. The X-Man-turned-child quickly settled into her new life there. She and Gambit worked as thieves, stealing from criminals and returning the goods to people who needed them.

But then, one evening at a local parade, Storm looked up from the floats and noticed a familiar

shape. It was Nanny's ship!

Suddenly, long tentacles descended from the craft, wrapping Gambit in an iron grip. In an instant, he was whisked up into the sky.

Storm flew after him, narrowly squeezing through the ship's door before it slammed shut.

I've been here before, Storm thought as she looked around in amazement. Memories came crashing back. Of how she had been an adult before Nanny kidnapped her. Of how she had been one of the X-Men. A *leader* of the X-Men!

Storm had to do something to save Gambit from the same fate. She charged into the main chamber, where Nanny had the Cajun chained to a wall.

"Release my friend!" Storm shouted as she let loose a punch—*KAPOW!*— that sent the Orphan Maker flying!

Nanny faced her, ray gun in hand.

"Wretched girl," said Nanny. "You've tried my patience for the last time!" She raised the gun...

A whooshing noise filled the room. Nanny spun around, but it was too late. A deadly

charged playing card—courtesy of Gambit—shot toward her.

Kaboom! The ship shuddered with the impact and went tumbling, crashing into the river below. The explosion freed Gambit from the chains. But the ship was sinking fast.

Gambit struggled to the surface with Storm in tow.

"Nanny! Orphan Maker!" sputtered Storm, gasping for breath. "We must dive back to the wreckage!"

"They are beyond our help, *petit,*" Gambit said gently. The two made their way to shore.

Storm was lost in thought. Finally she turned to Gambit. "Thank you for rescuing me," she said.

"And you, me," Gambit answered. "Remember what I said about sticking together? Well, I meant it, *chère.*"

Storm didn't try to correct him. She just smiled, and it was then that Gambit noticed she was changing. Now that Nanny had lost her power, Storm was returning to her adult self.

"You're...you're growing older!" said Gambit.

Storm gestured for the Cajun to follow her. "I am no longer the girl you befriended," she explained as they walked away from the river, from Nanny...and from their last tie to the Shadow King. "Tell me, Gambit. Have you heard of the X-Men?"

Gambit grinned. *X-Men*? Somehow, he knew this was the beginning of a wonderful friendship.